Maxwell   Sommerville

Engraved Gems

Maxwell   Sommerville

Engraved Gems

ISBN/EAN: 9783337624583

Printed in Europe, USA, Canada, Australia, Japan

Cover: Foto ©Andreas Hilbeck / pixelio.de

More available books at **www.hansebooks.com**

ENGRAVED GEMS

ENGRAVED GEMS

BY
MAXWELL SOMMERVILLE

PROFESSOR OF GLYPTOLOGY, UNIVERSITY OF PENNSYLVANIA;
AUTHOR OF "SANDS
OF SAHARA," "SIAM," ETC.; CORRESPONDING MEMBER OF THE
SOCIÉTÉ
ACADÉMIQUE DES SCIENCES, ARTS ET BELLES-LETTRES
DU DÉPARTEMENT DE L'AUBE,
FRANCE, ETC.

DREXEL BIDDLE, PUBLISHER
PHILADELPHIA LONDON
SAN FRANCISCOTORONTO

1901

6

PREFACE.

My former treatise, "Engraved Gems, their Place in the History of Art," being largely illustrated and inconvenient in size, I have abridged the work and with new material prepared this volume.

The various epochs of gem engraving from the earliest eras down to the XVIII. century are briefly described.

Many people throughout the year cast passing glances at my glyptic collection in the Free Museum of Science and Art of the University of Pennsylvania.

They express great admiration of the beautiful objects in stones of many colors and interesting designs.

It was never intended to make only an attractive display; what I have always desired and hoped for was that a proportion of our visitors would recognize in my life's work a contribution to science.

It is a classified representation of the glyptic work of more than forty centuries, so carefully arranged that those who care to learn through the medium of those beautiful engraved stones, cylinders, seals, and Gnostic tokens, may inform themselves intelligently on the science which these gems of all epochs so thoroughly exemplify.

Men in this Western World during the last three hundred years have been engrossed in the pursuit and acquisition of fortunes.

A fair proportion of the population now having secured competency, that condition once assured, with increased opportunities for intellectual culture and the enjoyment of art, the development of refined tastes and pursuits in America has been marked by the formation of many private collections. Amateurs have gradually become connoisseurs in manuscripts, ceramics, enamels, engravings, ancient coins, armor, and arms. Happily, each is engrossed in his particular branch of antiquities.

It is to be hoped that we may all profit by their researches, and that the antique objects acquired by them may be stored in the Archæological Museums of the world, that all who will may view them and learn from them.

MAXWELL SOMMERVILLE.

Presuming that the majority of my readers would understand the Latin inscription from an engraved stone, which decorates the cover of this book, I have not given any translation. By request I add the following explanation:

NON SOLVM NO I BIS NATI SVMVS I ORTVSQVE
        NOSTRI I PARTEM
PATRIA SI I BI VENDICAT PARTEM I PARENTES PARTEM
        AMICI I

    "Not alone for ourselves were we born, and of our
    birth our country claims for itself a part, our parents
    a part, our friends a part" (vendicat for vindicat).

On the reverse of the stone, which is not shown, is the inscription —

8

MORTIS MORES OMNIBUS ÆQUALES.

This is one of those peculiar maxims so often found in the
Latin language, as it is employed in epitaphs. The simplest
manner in which it can be translated is as follows:

$$\text{``The} \begin{Bmatrix} \text{manners} \\ \text{customs} \\ \text{usage} \\ \text{law} \end{Bmatrix} \text{of Death} \begin{Bmatrix} \text{are} \\ \text{is} \end{Bmatrix} \text{equal for all.''}$$

Death is here personified, as was Peace, Justice, Concord,
etc., by the Romans.

MAXWELL SOMMERVILLE.

CONTENTS.

LIST OF ILLUSTRATIONS.

14

ENGRAVED GEMS.

When specimens of any ancient art industry are brought together and classified in a museum it is interesting to compare each piece and trace the work from the hands of the different nationalities through all the transitions and changing history of past centuries.

My collection exemplifies the progress in execution of engraved gems from the most primitive eras through periods of varying excellence and of inevitable decline. The quality of the execution approaches perfection and degenerates as in a geometrical progression repeating itself in reverse; advancing and improving in fineness up to nearly the end of the first century, the century of Christ, and from the beginning of the second century retrograding to the base of mediocrity at the end of the fifth century.

The sixth and seventh centuries, the Byzantine period, yielded a group of principally religious cameos, abundant, curious, and of great interest.

This was succeeded by several hundred years not of repose in the art, but of wretched ignorance, when man almost ceased to create a connecting link in the history of the glyptic art. With rare exceptions, the specimens of that time

15

scarcely merit the designation of gems: it was a period that may be reasonably identified as the night of art, when, alas! in the darkness blows were stricken which destroyed and reduced to fragments much that was precious and beautiful, and vandalism, contributing nothing that was fair, robbed us of a large part of our inheritance.

The progression alluded to is, in my estimation, only a question of comparative beauty. If we seek for, or are capable of appreciating, the most interesting, that which gives us history, we must find it at the beginning of that progression —the era of the Babylonians—with its messages handed down to us on their wonderful cylinders.

My path of research has led me where are gathered stones— engraved stones, art-links in a carved chain reaching from the earliest cylinders and seals of the Persians, centuries before and beyond those wonderful stone books, the inscribed temples of Egypt.

Whilst considering and studying these specimens of the work of the ancients we will walk upon the crumbled ruins of by-gone centuries; our retrospective view shall be where changing elements, rust, and age have spared but traces of palaces and temples; we will stroll beside the pebbled course of a rapid stream until we reach a grove where I oft have been, and found a rich repast; no shrines, no obelisks, no statues, naught but these precious little stepping-stones, by which we will follow the stream of thus revealed history, and in the vale of antiquity, with these miniature monuments, study and enjoy the indelible portraiture of ages.

Palaces, obelisks, statues, and the walls of ancient cities have rarely been preserved to us, other than in decay, ruin, and fragments.

Yet engraved gems, those smaller monuments on hard stones, have been spared in the very débris of these larger structures, and we are thus enabled to secure examples of the handiwork of one branch of art, covering many epochs and periods.

My earnest eyes have looked up to and gazed upon the silent monuments and shrines of men, who during long centuries have rested from their scientific labors. A wanderer in lands adapted to my researches, my object has been to learn something of these mute monitors and to bring back to my native land examples of the special branch of ancient art which has been the pursuit of my life. Many discouraging moments, even years, have been passed, yet always with the hope that my labor and its results might some day be appreciated.

Years ago while rejoicing in the possession of the glyptic portraits of the Emperors Tiberius, Caracalla, Constantine, and that of Faustina, I thought with pleasant anticipation of the moment when on returning from voyages of acquisition I might introduce them to intellectual friends of "Science and Art."

These gems are here being considered in their respective epochs. Those who desire to inform themselves on the science of "Engraved Gems" will find in these pages a brief view of that subject; it is in response to many friendly demands, and shall be as concise as reasonably possible, in keeping with ancient records on engraved stones, cylinders, and seals. Your attention is asked to this general view of the subject, with the hope that it may enlist some inquirers and admirers of this glyptic question, so little esteemed or understood in these days; a subject not only representing a branch of art covering a period of forty odd centuries, but a science through whose engraved gems we have been enabled to enrich our knowledge of the ancient history of the world.

Each nation which in ancient times practised the glyptic art, produced a certain style or quality of execution.

After serious study of the general subject of glyptology, one finds that the work of each epoch, and of each nationality, bears some unmistakable trait. These features we can almost always recognize as emanating from a certain people.

So completely have we acquired an acquaintance with the various characteristics of each nation's handiwork in engraving gems, that we are enabled also to discern the epoch; not to a year, but within a century or even a decade.

In proportion to the rudeness of the incisions we recognize the barbaric condition of the people among whom they were incised; also in proportion to the fineness of the incision, beauty of conception, and execution of the design, do we estimate the civilization of the epoch and of the people.

Some of the nations who have bequeathed us engraved gems were, in two respects, the first sculptors. They were first, not only because none of ability had preceded them, but rather were they first in art rank, and in excellence of conception; their execution has never been surpassed; their statues and high reliefs have never been equalled in modern times.

Many of those colossal art works in stone have been transported to the Vatican, to France, England, Austria, Germany, Russia, some even to America; we are all conversant with them. Therefore, you can readily imagine how we define and classify the work of each epoch and nation, when a miscellaneous mass of engraved gems are placed before us for classification.

EGYPT.

Everyone in these days is familiar with those colossal stone figures of Rameses, Osiris, Thotmes, and others in the sands of Egypt. Their heavy, placid countenances, almost seeming to dream, while their inert arms and hands hold forth the insignia of autocrats of Egypt under the Pharaohs.

In Egypt, especially in the earlier or more remote dynasties, man seems to have had the intention of handing down to posterity the records of his power, his possessions, and of his own appearance, on great stone statues, obelisks, and basso-rilievos, in the most indestructible manner.

Besides the colossal stone bequests created for generations unborn, happily they produced the same portraitures and cartouches in miniature gems. The majority of the temple decorations in stone have crumbled, while we can possess and enjoy the glyptic relics which have survived the ravages of time uninjured.

SOMMERVILLE COLLECTION.

467

480 obverse.

489 obverse.

458

480 reverse.

489 reverse.

456

EGYPTIAN.

Among the Scarabei are especially interesting examples larger in size termed funereal; No. 1476 in my University Collection is one of those Scarabei which were buried with the dead, sometimes on the breast underneath the

21

wrappings, and sometimes within the body of the mummy in the place of the heart. The heart was embalmed separately in a vase, and placed under the protection of the genius Duaoumautew. This doubtlessly was done because the heart was considered indispensable for the resurrection, yet it could not be placed in the body until it had been upon the scales and had passed the judgment of Osiris. When the sentence was favorable it was promised that "his heart shall be returned to its original cavity." The heart, the principle of existence and regeneration, was symbolized by the Scarabeus. This is why texts relative to the heart were inscribed on funereal Scarabei. On this Scarabeus the deceased speaks, saying: "I hope that my soul shall speedily quit or rise from the regions infernal, and, reappearing on earth, may do all that pleases it."

Also No. 1479, a funereal Scarabeus, interesting from the fact that the inscription contains part of the 30th chapter of the Book of the Dead—that is, the chapter concerning the heart: "My heart, which comes to me from my mother—my heart, necessary to my existence on earth—do not raise thyself against me among or before the chief divinities." These were the superior gods, whom the Egyptians supposed to be in the immediate surrounding or presence of Isis.

The remainder of the inscription is less legible. On the first line is the name of Osiris Jam (all the dead had Osiris prefixed to their names); on the last line is the name of his father, which is indistinct; it was evidently the same as the name of a plant, and ending with M, but cannot be defined; that is, it is inscribed "son of — —," and then the unintelligible name alluded to.

Also No. 1457, a funereal Scarabeus, on which the deceased, speaking, expresses hopes, continually repeated, that his soul may have a happy voyage, happy relief, and transport from the inevitable transitory domain to which all are consigned.

Also No. 1480, Egyptian Scarabeus, containing a vow or wish, a vase representing a libation. The sum of the rendering of the inscription is: "I dedicate my life to truth, and hope for cooling breezes and libations."

And No. 1461. The inscription expresses a vow or wish: "NEFER KHET NEB"—"All things good (for thee)!"—a New Year's wish.

There were artisans who engraved the larger funereal Scarabei and kept them ready made on sale, so that in the event of a man dying unexpectedly in youth or the prime of life who had not thought to prepare for his sojourn in the tomb, his family repaired to these shops, and, choosing a Scarabeus to their taste or liking, purchased it; the engraver then added the name of the deceased, and they placed it under the wrappings of the mummy.

These traffickers also did a thriving trade with the living: many provided themselves in advance. There were always a variety from which to choose; the engraver had them for every taste. They were inscribed with just such vows or wishes for the future and the repose or the enjoyment of the soul, or the commending of the soul to the patronage and protection of some special god or deess, as the case might demand for a man or a woman. Often selections were given from the poetic devotional writings of their mentors, and frequently we meet with selections from the Book of the Dead.

We find shreds and examples of the costumes of the occupants of graves of other ancient nations. These garments were made, as now, that the body might be decorously placed at rest. This we also find in Egypt, the mummy-wrappings concealing and protecting the Scarabei presenting this beautiful sentiment, indeed unique—a symbol that was worn in life, emblematic of its ephemeral tenure and of the ultimate resurrection from death and the grave; a symbol that accompanied its owner to the narrow home, not to ornament it, but as a token of that tenant's belief that this would be only a brief occupancy; a symbol ready to be worn when that tenant should enter on his resurrection into an eternal lease of joy in a world beyond.

PERSIA AND BABYLON.

We are particularly interested in the curious and elaborately engraved cylinders and seals of the Assyrians, Persians, the Babylonians, the Chaldeans, the Hittites, which not only give us their costumes, but are laden with cuneiform inscriptions. In my collection there is a gem of the same style of work as the stone slab in the University Museum procured by Professor H. V. Hilprecht from the ancient palace of Ashurna Sirbal, King of Assyria 884 to 860 B. C.

This glyptic specimen is in miniature, engraved on a rich wine-colored dark sard bearing a portrait of King Sapor I.; he was the second of the Sassanians, who reigned in the third century. He was crowned in the year 242 A. D. It is surrounded by an inscription in Sassanian. Sapor's invasion of Palmyra and his contests with the forces of Zenobia are interesting incidents of that romantic episode in Oriental history.

PERSIAN AND SASSANIAN SEALS.

Cylinders are evidently the oldest form of seals, though it is believed that the art originated on sections of wooden reeds. We find Chaldean cylinders now more than 4000 years old.

The signets of kings in the cylindric form were incised in the harder and more precious materials, such as chalcedony in several hues, the fairest those tinged with a sapphire tint (though not the most ancient), sards, carnelians, and occasionally beautiful red jasper; hematite in abundance; serpentine and many softer stones, alabaster, steatite, etc.

It remains a question on what materials the impressions were made, though scientists have learned that the figures in relief on patties of pipe-clay found so plentifully in Babylon are the imprints of these cylinders.

Though a large proportion of cylinders are rudely designed and more coarsely executed, many of them are freely, vigorously, and well drawn, evincing a high degree of talent.

Remark the anatomical drawings of man and beast; they are unsurpassed in any age, especially the contest between men and lions, where naturally the muscles are strongly developed and show prominently.

As bearers of messages from that remote period, they come more welcome to us than the fairest Greek or Roman intaglios.

With an interesting pictured and lettered cylinder in hand one may have before him one of the keys to the most ancient fountain-heads in which history is locked up. My taste has grown and perhaps been influenced by long association with such gems, until I now often find more pleasure in regarding a rude fragment of Assyrian work than I did thirty years ago when I sought only the beautiful.

The place of these Babylonian cylinders in the history of art cannot be classed as decorative, for as they were originally used only as seals, and mostly business or official signets, they were not at that time used to decorate the person, though they were worn on necklaces and bracelets by the ancient Greeks.

No. 499 in my collection is one of the most interesting because the great and lamented François Lenormant examined it with me, wrote his opinion, and expressed his admiration of it.

It is a Babylonian cylinder, 29 millimetres broad by 3 millimetres in length. On it is represented a seated god with a two-horned head-dress in a long flounced dress; before him an altar with four spreading legs, an antelope, a small walking figure, a scorpion, two birds facing one another; other human figures.

Lenormant wrote while attending a seance of l'Institut de France.

SOMMERVILLE COLLECTION.

1403

1405

498

499

1374

IMPRESSIONS OF BABYLONIAN CYLINDERS.

SOMMERVILLE COLLECTION.

ASSYRIAN.
1366

PERSIAN.
1402

HITTITE.
1401

30

PHŒNICIAN.
495

CYPRIAN.
1370

IMPRESSIONS OF ASSYRIAN, PERSIAN, HITTITE,
PHŒNICIAN, AND CYPRIAN CYLINDERS.

"This cylinder which appears to be of serpentine belongs incontestably to the most antique epoch of Chaldean art of the first years of the ancient empire. It is at least contemporaneous with those cylinders bearing the names of the oldest kings of d'Ous and like those of the Dungi."

Persia and Assyria furnish us also a beautiful series of seals; the earlier conical, then a series of spherical seals, with one side flattened, on which is the design and inscription, and then the later Sassanian, also spherical, yet more flattened on the sides, which are pierced, and whose circumferences are beautifully ornamented.

There exist a large series of subjects adopted by their owners on account of their superstitious belief in their talismanic virtues; and quite a series of rudely-drawn animals emblematic of vigilance, fidelity, courage, strength, etc. Sometimes on seals as well as on cylinders a full-length figure is given in whose costume there is a marked peculiarity of drapery, the folds crossing the form diagonally, like a Burmese Sarong.

They are on a great variety of chalcedonies, sards, jaspers, and other beautiful stones of color.

Those of the Assyrians, dating as far back as 1110 B. C., resemble in form the bells herdsmen hang upon their grazing cattle that they may hear them when they have strayed.

The location of the ancient Persians in proximity to India, whose river-beds were rich in varieties of hard water-worn pebbles, enabled them to procure from thence suitable stones for decoration and for inscriptions. Thousands of these decorated and inscribed stones have been unearthed and are to-day in our possession; glyptologists can and have read them. Many examples of these cylinders, seals, and their imprints are before you.

It is proven that the Assyrians knew of and practiced the art of engraving on stone; we are not fully convinced that they were the first to practice the art.

We are frequently able to corroborate glyptic inscriptions by statements in Holy Writ, though we certainly find on ancient cylinders, incisions many centuries anterior to the records to which we have here alluded.

We know little of the Assyrian divinities through ancient manuscripts, yet we have volumes about their deities written on the cylinders of Babylon and Nineveh. They were seldom in metallic mountings, but, being pierced with holes, were strung on cords and worn on the wrist and neck.

There is a host of occupants of the Assyrian heaven, with Asshur the supreme god, Beltis Mylitta the great mother, etc.; and on the seals in sard and chalcedony we have sacred doves, lions, horses, etc., and a winged bull, Nin, the god of hunting, etc.

These intaglio seals were often used as locks; the doors of wine-cellars were secured by placing a seal upon them. Cylinders have also been made by several races of South American Indians, and are still to be seen in Brazil.

BABYLONIAN CYLINDERS, THE SOURCE OF HISTORY.

We have a most interesting and instructive illustration of the value of modern research among the relics of antiquity in the fact that in 1854, Sir Henry Rawlinson, in deciphering the inscriptions on some cylinders found in the ruins of Um-Kir (the ancient Ur of the Chaldees), made historical discoveries in regard to the last King of Babylon that

34

confirmed the truth of the book of Daniel, and harmonized discrepancies between Holy Scripture and profane history which up to that time had been hopelessly irreconcilable.

Among the bequests from Persia many gems are engraved on the hardest and most precious stones; they present us with portraits of their monarchs, deities, legends, religious creeds, and seals of office. Though rude, they are exceedingly interesting from their antiquity and as being the achievements of a people so remote from the European centre of civilization.

THE ETRUSCANS—ETRURIA.

The country of the ancient Etruscans was north from the Tiber to the Ciminian Forest and the Tolfa Mountains.

They have bequeathed us a mass of gems, a large proportion in the form of Scarabei, and many really fine intaglios, which were not only used as seals, but served as decorations, both in finger-rings and as brooches for women. The Etruscan tombs have yielded many Scarabei in mountings of virgin gold, sometimes the precious metal twisted, again corrugated; also some ornamental gold work as brooches. The sard and chalcedony beetles usually had an engraved beaded margin, and were revolvable, being set on a pivot which was attached to a frame generally oval in form.

The Etruscans, unlike their predecessors, have left us few examples other than the very gems and Scarabei by which to study their glyptic work. We have the decorations of their sepulchral homes; we know of their costumes by their mural paintings in those subterranean chambers.

Their glyptic style is unique; a series of deeply-drilled cavities, afterward joined to one another, forming designs frequently contorted by the artist in his endeavor to bring his subject into the very limited space of the under face of the Scarabeus.

ETRUSCAN.

The Etruscans probably borrowed the idea of the Scarabeus form of gem from the Egyptians; they certainly shaped it more beautifully. They seem to have adopted only the symbol.

There was a difference in the quality of their Scarabei corresponding with the classes or stations in the life of the people; those cut for royalty, nobility, or the wealthy naturally received more attention in forming and finishing.

Those for the tradespeople, the well-to-do, we find quite a distinctive order. In this group they are less graceful in shape, the beetles are rounder, thicker, and shorter, not so carefully finished, as also the simpler borders formed of two lines just within the edge, either crossed with regular, straight, or oblique lines forming bars, with some little variety of pattern.

The Etruscans called themselves the Rasenna; the early Italians knew them as the Tusci or Etrusci. The Greeks denominated the race as Turrhenoi or Tursenoi, and the ancient Latin name was Tursci.

The engraved records of the Etruscans have hitherto successfully defied all attempts at interpretation. Now that the Assyrian and Egyptian records have been read, these Etruscan inscriptions present the only considerable philological problem that still remains unsolved. But that it remains unsolved has not been for want of effort. A vast amount of ingenuity and of erudition has been wasted in attempts to explain the inscriptions by the aid of Latin, Greek, Hebrew, Phœnician, Arabic, Ethiopic, Chinese, Coptic, and Basque have all been tried in vain.

It may be safely affirmed that few of these attempts have been regarded as satisfactory by any person except their authors.

A comparison of the Etruscan inscriptions with the characters of the Finno-Turkic language, a form of speech employed by those inhabiting the region lying between the Ural and the Altai Mountains, has, I believe, resulted with the first and only success that has ever attended such investigations.

SOMMERVILLE COLLECTION.

548

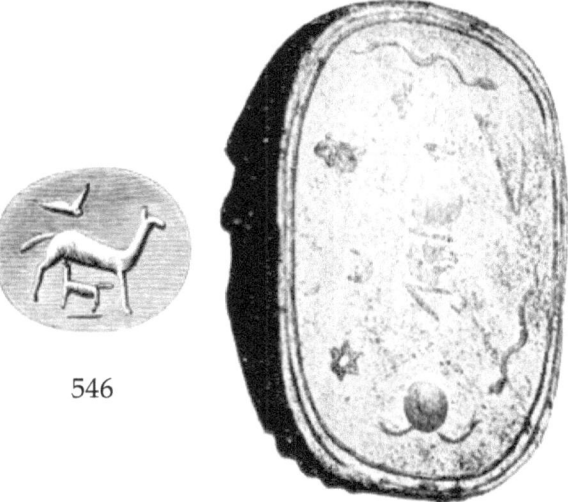

546

553

558

40

555

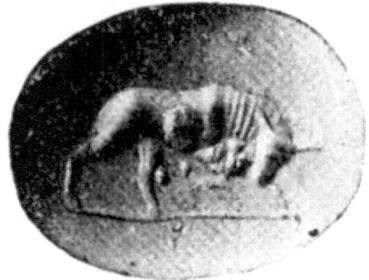

554

PHŒNICIAN SCARABEI AND INTAGLIOS.

PHŒNICIA.

Alas, we have to dig deep and toil to learn all we want to know so much about these people who 2500 years ago inhabited that narrow mountain-guarded strip of land looking westward on the same emerald sea that to-day breaks on the shore of what is now Syria.

They have consigned us no books, no pamphlets, no journals, not a page—only here and there do we unearth a graven stone, an inscribed cylinder and Scarabeus; and with these stone fragments of that nation's literary bequests we will hope to obtain some idea of the history of Phœnicia—Phœnicia, whose people, not content with mounting five thousand feet to the temple of the Casian Jupiter, to see the sun upon the morning horizon, floated away on their frail barks on the deep waters, seeking light, knowledge, and gain. Mythology was their religion, which, like the subjects and styles of their engraved stones and gems of iridescent antique paste, was borrowed from Assyria, Greece, and even somewhat from the myths of the people among whom many of them settled.

Herodotus speaks of the Phœnicians as a branch of the Semitic or Aramæan nations; they originally dwelt on the shores of the Erythrean Sea. They also occupied islands in the Persian Gulf, among others Aradus and Tylus, where temples in Phœnician architecture were found; and it is known that the Phœnicians left these islands and colonized in the Ægean and Mediterranean Seas before the time of Joshua, 1444 B. C.

Of the Romans and the Grecians, we have their history through the writings of their own historians; and of the Egyptians, by their monuments teeming with hieroglyphics, history, and theology. Of the Phœnicians little is extant in writings from their own people; we are dependent on what other nations have recorded—in fact, what we know of them may be called tradition. The Phœnicians were termed "the merchants of many isles." We can hardly say they cultivated the arts at home, for wherever they went, there they made their home; on every island inhabited by them are found evidences of their industry as gem-cutters— intaglios, scarabei, and seals. I remember how I was impressed on going ashore at Syra and walking through its beautiful amphitheatral city of to-day, whose site had once known those very Phœnicians, examples of whose gems may be seen in my collection.

They emigrated as far west as Sardinia. Sardinia was originally called Sandaleotis, from its form, which resembles a human foot or its imprint, where during centuries a moderate harvest has been reaped of gems emanating from their handiwork.

SOMMERVILLE COLLECTION.

1810

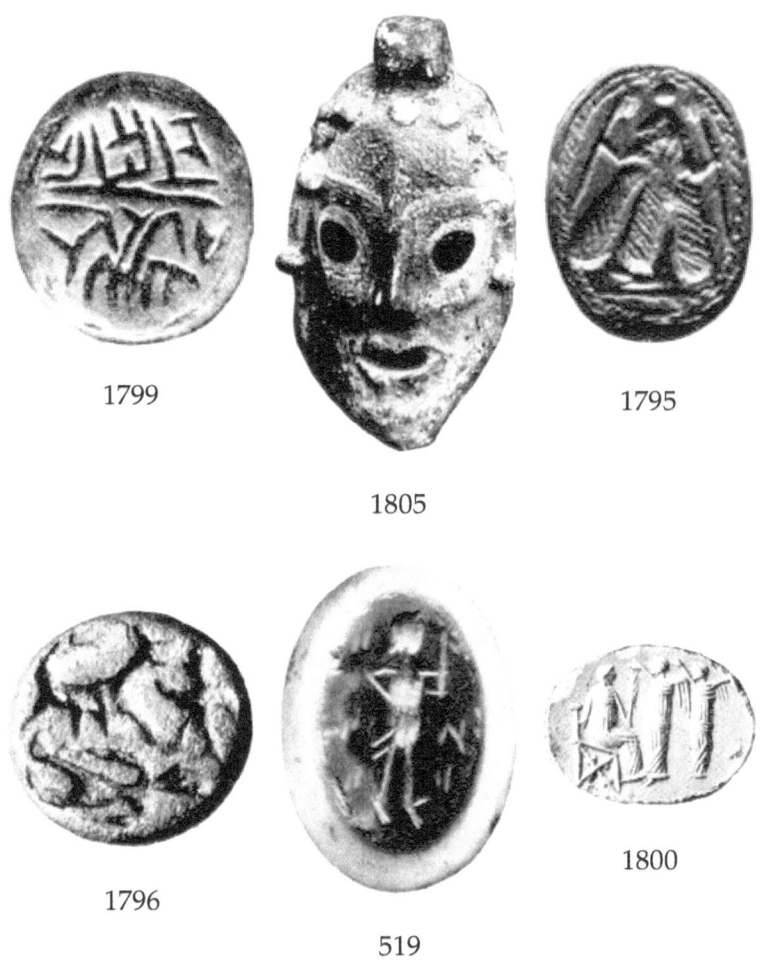

1799

1795

1805

1796

519

1800

PHŒNICIA.

To a practised eye their work is distinguishable from that of other nations; the touch, drawing, execution, and the distinctive character of their subjects render them readily recognizable. Yet the symbolic characters are not entirely distinctive, for they often clearly indicate imitation of Assyrian and Egyptian work and design. For that reason it is often difficult to decide or classify gem-objects found in many of the islands once colonized by them, from the very fact that in design they at times lack originality.

They were a migratory people, and in this brief glance at the whole range of our subject we shall be satisfied with mention of their colony at Tharros, on the island at Sardinia, where the most unquestionably authentic Phœnician Scarabei have been found in excavations made during the last sixty years. They are principally cut on green jasper, and in character resemble Persian designs.

In these times we write our history every day on millions of great pages of white paper. In almost no contingency will future generations have any difficulty of learning who we were, where we came from, how we have formed the master metal—iron—into thousands of implements and instruments, or how they have been employed; being supplied with our ready inscribed history, they can begin where we have left off and profit by our experience.

GREECE.

The earliest specimens of Greek gems bore traces of Egyptian style; they represented objects rather symbolically than by artistic delineation of the beautiful in the human form or in nature. On the box of Cypselus death was represented with crooked legs, beauty and youth by long tresses of hair, power by long hands, swiftness and agility by long feet. Many of the oldest Greek statues were accompanied with the names of the subjects represented, which seems to imply that the artist was conscious of his deficiency, both in character and expression. Yet in time they created single figures and groups in fair marble, whose symmetry and exquisite modelling of the human form command the admiration of all. They are either at rest or displaying the muscles, sinews, and even the passions of athletic men and adorable women.

Greece was the source of the finest and richest glyptic art-treasures in a decorative sense. Grecian intaglios are of superb execution, of exquisite fineness and finish. This superiority can in a measure be accounted for by the encouragement the profession received from the nation, both from rulers and from the people.

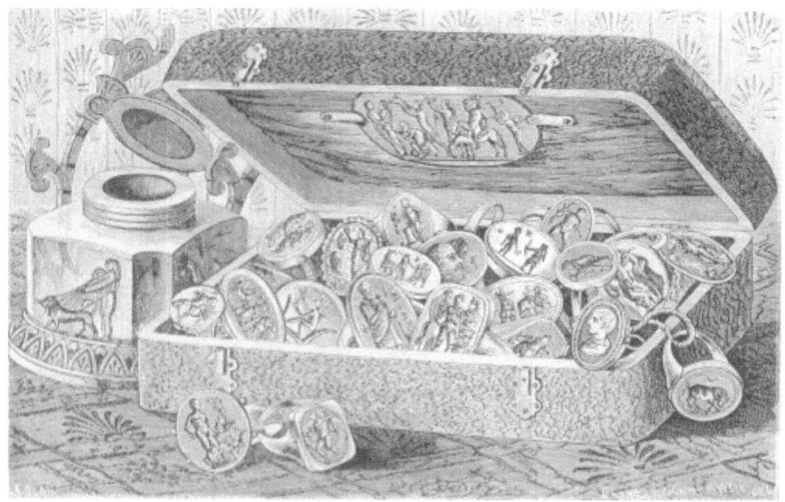

GREEK AND ROMAN INTAGLIO RINGS.

In proportion to the extended cultivation of taste and the increased demand, the ranks of the incisori were repleted. Among so many contestants rivalry and emulation had a very happy effect in forming and creating artists who were indeed eminent, and whose works even to-day sparkle as jewel-gems in the diadem which crowns the history of their place in art.

The perfect finish, polish, and detail of their choicest examples render them superior to the gems of any other people, even to many that come from Roman sources.

It is often almost impossible intelligently to explain the difference between the gems of the Greeks and the Romans;

such power of distinguishing one from the other is only to be gained by long observation and close study of the subject.

Many of them, however, seem to say to us whenever we meet them in exile, "We are of Ancient Greece, Grecians of the epoch and home of Pericles the patron, and Phidias the practitioner." We are reminded of these classic, silent monuments when we meet and recognize the strictly glyptic work of the incisori of the land of the Parthenon. It is by comparison and contrast that we study and classify their gems. Beautiful stones have recently been discovered at Mycenæ, among which are engraved gems bearing effigies of animals curiously and artistically drawn, and which, by their Oriental style, prove that the ancient Greeks, who bequeathed so much to their successors, also inherited art-models from a people 1000 years B. C.

At first the colonists incised what was known as the Hellenic style, and then, as they fraternized with the Romans, and as the Romans made incisions under the Greek teaching, their glyptic works showed the Greek influence, and such works constituted the gems of the Græco-Romano. Many of the intaglios by Romans, of this school, were signed in Greek characters, and can be seen in my collection. This act of a Roman signing his name in characters other than the Latin letters peculiar to his own country shows how Grecian art was appreciated in the Græco-Roman epoch.

GRÆCO-ROMAN.

ROMAN.

The classic multitudinous gems of the Roman period: their emperors, statesmen, warriors, and poets—in fact, some of their gems have given to us the only perfect portraits in miniature that have been preserved from ancient time; incidents of their conflicts, their sports, games, and apparel —with the mass of chimeras and at times mysteries. The endless grand historical cameos, some of which in my collection represent nineteen and even twenty-two figures in good relief carefully engraved on a single stone. We know that gem-engraving in Rome in the prolific period was celebrated for the greatest diversity of subjects both in cameos and intaglios. Rome, the patroness of the ancient world.

Rome did not achieve this phenomenal position unaided, though in its palmiest days it was the art shrine of the nations. To attain this position it drew from comparatively distant sources, and borrowed talent wherever it was available.

When Rome's reputation as the glyptic school was heralded and established throughout the nations as the art centre of the world, it became as we have inferred, the vortex into which hosts of artisans were attracted, and who, when once there, established themselves.

They were well received; were elated with plenty of occupation, emolument, and good prices; in their new life they identified themselves with their fellow incisori, and became Romans, or, at least, Græco-Romans.

In fact, the variety in styles and designs produced by all the ancient peoples of Italy was due to emigration. Profiting by the culture and art experience of Etruria, Rome learned from the Etruscan architects, potters, die-sinkers, and gem-engravers.

They learned from these more ancient incisori many useful lessons which enabled them to accomplish wonders. Within the limited space available on those little gem stones, they depicted with complicated minuteness details of events in actual history, and displayed remarkable tact and astonishing powers of composition in their rendering of groups of figures and mythological deities in scenes of quasi historical events.

Though we have seen the work of the Græco-Romans bearing evidence of combined influence and instruction, there was even at that very epoch a school, or powerful class of artists, in Rome, who retained their own individuality, who were Romans of Rome, and from whose hands, and from their successors, we have inherited grand cameos and intaglios, portraying their emperors, statesmen, philosophers, mythological subjects, and occasionally groups recording important events in Roman history.

Considering we find Roman glyptic work of merit until nearly the close of the second century A. D., there was in all a period of good gem-engraving covering about eight hundred years.

Throughout all this time the glyptic art flourished under the protection of kings and emperors, who for the general encouragement of the civilizing arts, served their own interests and gratified their tastes for luxury and the beautiful by their constant patronage of gem-engraving.

ABRAXAS.

The unique mystic gems of the Gnostics, known as the Abraxas, are a series by themselves; they had no prototype.

Their strangely decorated and inscribed stone tokens are so characteristic of the sect that they also are easily recognized. The task of explaining the meaning of these incisions is the more difficult, as the veil is almost impenetrable which obscures the history of everything that pertains to these little stone fetiches of the Gnostics.

The very disciples who carried those amuletic gems did so without understanding the meaning of the marks and symbols engraved upon them. They evidently were sacred types of their superstitious creed, invented and placed there by their mentors or priests.

They were Pagans, Jews, and nominal Christians, and we find in their inexhaustible inscriptions a series of emblems, Hebrew and Syriac, which dimly show forth Christ the Son, and Sun of Righteousness with AΔONAI, and the seven Greek vowels symbolic of the seven heavens. These Greek vowels have often amused me when I have shown an Abraxas talisman with long inscription to some Greek scholar not acquainted with their gems, who would stumble when he reached the other characters.

SOMMERVILLE COLLECTION.

574 obverse.

574 reverse.

562 obverse.

562 reverse.

564 obverse.

569

564 reverse.

573 obverse.

573 reverse.

ABRAXAS OR GNOSTIC GEMS.

The religion of Jesus Christ was by no means established peaceably and immediately in the days following his crucifixion and resurrection. By a close reading of several of the Epistles of the New Testament you will see that during the first and second centuries many were the beliefs and even schisms among those who thought that they believed in Christ. In the second Epistle to the Corinthians there is evidence that the learned doctors raised altar in opposition to altar. None of them were avowedly reared by the Gnostics, yet the Apostle Paul recognized their opposition to the orthodox growing faith and combated them, knowing that Christianity at that critical moment was constantly losing adherents who, through the sophistries of the Abraxas, were daily relinquishing their ardent hold on the new hope in Christ.

Undoubtedly this Abraxas sect, who made so many cabalistic talismans, which were so blindly accepted and worn by their disciples, had among them many who knew of our Saviour. It appears from history, and from their mystic characters, that they had a clearer appreciation of

Christ than a just or reasonable fear of the prince of the region of darkness, as Zoroaster termed the chief of inferno. They derived their idea of Satan, the arch tempter, from the appellation given him by certain sects in Central Asia, where, to better deceive their victims, they spoke of him as an angel of light. In modern times the lives of many men have proved that they had no desire to repulse Satan, but rather lived harmoniously in fellowship with him as their guide.

St. Paul besought the Christians to guard well the precious truths revealed and confided to them, and to fear and fly from the profane novelties that were threatening the welfare of their souls (I. Timothy, vi).

In a word, these great pagan monuments were the forerunners and the models of many of the small and portable talismans that were freely disseminated by the priests of the Abraxas to their disciples and their followers.

One important fact must be understood. The signs, symbols, the unintelligible hieroglyphs of the Gnostics, the Basilidians, which we find on the Abraxas gems—almost all talismans—are the mystic representations of a sect thus made up of people of several nations, all of whom in their aspirations sought for knowledge of the invisible power, that unquestionably had created and who governed all things, whom, though unseen, they served and feared.

SOMMERVILLE COLLECTION.

561
obverse.

561 reverse.

1431

568
obverse.

568 reverse.

565

ABRAXAS OR GNOSTIC GEMS.

EARLY CHRISTIANS.

The events narrated in the New Testament of our Lord Jesus Christ resulted in the drawing together of his followers, who daily sought to worship their risen Redeemer, notwithstanding the terrible opposition of the heathen autocrats of Rome.

Very naturally in proportion to the imperial opposition the faithful became more fervent. As they could not publicly meet for worship and prayer, they were compelled to do so clandestinely.

Now in order that only the faithful should enter, and that the enemies might be detected, a system of tesseræ was invented, and soon these were made in the form of engraved pietradura; the designs always were of the simplest character —a dove, two or three fish, two palms crossed, etc., and other religious gem-tokens; this formed the glyptic epoch known as the Early Christian gems.

Be it understood, there was no representation of "God," the "Father," or of "Christ;" only simple symbols of the class already described; symbols of their simple faith.

This was a period of glyptic work in which a series of gems were engraved by a people who pursued their avocation under peculiarly trying circumstances; they were the "Early Christians."

The children born of those who had already espoused the new doctrine were taught with the first lessons of life to know, to revere, and to trust in the Saviour; with their earliest lisping words, from the cradle they learned to plead in prayer for divine protection.

The earliest Christians, the first converts, born in paganism, had not the opportunities with which their offspring and descendants were favored; they had to renounce the superstitions in which they had been reared, and were often obliged to sever the friendly ties of youth.

These first enrolled with the followers of Christ, pagans, whose convictions impelled them to accept the Redeemer, offered to their inquiring hearts, commenced anew lives with many pagan prejudices and customs clinging to them.

Some of them were incisori, and it is interesting to observe among the comparatively few gems of this epoch the evidence of transition. Many of these gems unquestionably bearing some of the simpler Christian decoration were still adorned with pagan designs. On one we find Astarte; on others, Serapis, Mercury, Venus, or Apollo. The divinity, the loveliness of expression sometimes given to these transition portraits seem to have been the work of artists whose souls were imbued with the singular beauty of that Divine Man whom Publius Lentulus announced to the Senate as "the prophet of truth," a man whose personal beauty excelled all human creatures—and yet the effigy really was of some pagan deity. These gems, however, which were characterized by remnants of pagan decoration, were only of the epoch immediately succeeding the institution of the sect of "followers of Christ," and preceding the dawning struggle of the "Early Christians," to establish their belief and to retain their rights as citizens. They renounced the idolatrous religion of the nation, and their glyptic work was generally typical of the purity and simplicity of their faith and their devotion to its observance.

BYZANTINE.

One might naturally suppose that the gems of the early Christians would abound in representations of scriptural events and incidents of the life of Christ. Such was not the case; these subjects were abundantly produced by the Byzantines about the fifth century A. D. This can be accounted for from the fact that most of these subject-gems were engraved to decorate the sacred vessels and paraphernalia of the church altars in Byzantium.

With Constantine we find the Byzantine epoch in its maturity. With the simplicity of the early Christians we have remarked that everything like representation of the Godhead was eliminated or rather forbidden.

It was the Byzantines who created for the gem market token cameos and intaglios on which were incised effigies of the Holy Family, and incidents in every phase in that series of events that never has been equalled in historic interest in the records of time: the birth, life, trial, sufferings, death, and resurrection of the Son of God.

Elaborate details characterized the cameos picturing the triumphs of that Christian emperor and the portraiture of his mother Helena.

SOMMERVILLE COLLECTION.

589

580

590

578

575

BYZANTINE CHRIST.

The annunciation, the visitation, the birth in the manger, the adoration of the wise men and the magi, the bearing of the cross, the crucifixion, etc.

With the Byzantine epoch we meet with the Emperor Constantine as we turn from the first period of decadence, in fact, almost demise, of the art of the incisori.

The justice, energy, and enterprise of Constantine showered benefits on all industrious men in the Eastern Roman world. Skilled workmen, spared from the absorbing conflicts of war, anew devoted themselves in peace to their mechanical avocations.

Prosperity ruled and was assured to the people. Foremost among these artisans were the gem-engravers; the demand for their glyptic productions, and the amount produced, was phenomenal.

The dignity of Constantine's successful empire was sustained by a retinue of courtiers; luxury characterized all the imperial decorations of his palace.

His willing subjects supplied his demands and gratified his refined tastes by zealously executing his liberal commands in all branches of art, and especially in the art of gem-engraving, which contributed largely to the court adornment.

Recognizing the near relationship between gems and coins, we here see that Constantine, shortly after he had established his empire in Byzantium, removed the pagan emblems from the coins of the empire, and issued others on which he caused to be impressed the legend illustrating and recording the peculiar incident of his conversion; to this was added a phœnix, emblematic of the renovation of his empire, together with the monogram of Christ, and the Angel of Victory, which in his vision had directed his course at the time of his conversion to Christianity and triumph over the pagan enemy.

At the time of his baptism at Nicomedia he clad himself in a white robe, and from that time he never resumed the imperial purple.

This incident was also engraved, and formed the subject of a design on a later coin.

The engravers employed by Constantine were incisori of the highest rank of that period; none others were in favor. They executed portraits of his family, of his wife Fausta, of his sons, and of himself—in combat, in bust, on horseback, in imperial power; always laureated, and principally on cameos, very few intaglios being cut at this time.

Several important examples have survived the rack and ruin of time, and may be seen in the Bibliothèque Nationale at Paris, the British Museum at London, the Royal and Imperial Collections of Vienna and St. Petersburg, and in my collection.

These unique gems, those commissioned by Constantine, however, form a small proportion of the glyptic harvest from the Byzantine period. With Constantine commences the series of scriptural cameos, which continue during several years in Byzantia.

The great number of cameos preserved from this epoch bearing scriptural subjects, which were ordered and engraved for reliquaries and every description of vessels, and for the adornment of altar book-bindings, for church and cathedral ceremonies, far exceeds in quantity those imperial portraits, and to an appreciator of distinctive specialties in a representative art collection they are more interesting.

BYZANTINE.

After a few heads of Christ attributed to the Sassanians, we meet in the reign of Constantine the first gem portraits of our Saviour. These sacred portraits, even at times rudely rendered, have often more divinity in them than many similar subjects of a later period.

The distinctive, most characteristic, Byzantine gems are the large series of scriptural cameos, designed in relief for the ornamentation of the sacred vessels and other paraphernalia on the altars of the churches at the Byzantine capital.

MEDIÆVAL.

The era in the decline in art was sensibly marked in the glyptic branch. The very rude and often grotesquely drawn designs we meet in this long period, the Middle Ages, may well be termed the dark days.

The eras of art in the history of nations have been marked by the same changing characteristics; light has invariably been succeeded by darkness; there are shadows ever following the bright rays of the sun. This day of imagery and sculpture, feeble at its dawn, radiant in its morning, powerful in the glory and effulgence of its meridian, deteriorated as evening advanced, faded in the twilight, was at last veiled in the long period of decadence—the Middle Ages, the night of art.

These people, so credulous and so trusting in these token-stones, by degrees formed themselves into groups, at first of two or three, with ties of pious friendship; subsequently these associations gradually increased in the numbers of their adherents until the growing fanatic idea of closing one's eyes on the sinful world was the incentive which formed at first asylums, and soon after monasteries; and the monastic life became popular; wavering men, feeling themselves too weak to face the temptations of the world, resorted to these holy retreats and there sought God. Few reasonable men can be truly happy without occupation, and, happily for us, these recluses saw the importance and the historic interest of engraved gems. Many interesting intaglios were thus spared from loss and destruction.

The numerous orders of monks during this barbarous epoch collected all that possibly could be saved from the destroying avalanche, and with great diligence transcribed on parchment types of the existing literature.

The laborers in the limited field of art in the Middle Ages were these dwellers in monasteries. To them we are indebted for some rude fibres in the fabric with which this period of darkness is canopied; they walked under it in the simplicity of monastic life; and to us at least it conveys the lesson that man has forgotten so much, knows so little, and has so much to learn.

Their intaglios were generally of a spiritual and devotional character, though some of them relieved the tedium of cloister life by creating in *basso-rilievo* on bone and ivory the most ludicrous and mirth-provoking designs.

The subjects of the engraved gems of the eighth, ninth, tenth, and eleventh centuries are to a great extent unmeaning figures and heads—portraits of unknown personages, now and then reproductions of ancient Roman emperors and military heroes of historic renown, yet poorly rendered and bad in execution.

There are also many inexplicable subjects, portraying groups of three four, five, and six figures, evidently intended to commemorate events in history; also mythological processions, both in rude intaglios and equally mediocre cameos, giving triumphs of Silenus and Bacchus, portraying these heroes in forms, the drawing of which would raise blushes on their cheeks could they return to earth and be allowed to criticise their effigies. Silenus, even full of wine, would have growled and remonstrated, and would have pronounced some of them absurd misrepresentations; they, however, are very interesting, if only on account of their contrast with the examples of Greek and Roman glyptic art.

In this epoch, again, we find instances of the sensitiveness of the numismatic branch of the art of gem-engraving, for the models of all pieces of money are intaglios, and thus far they are related to the glyptic art; and it has always been the first industry giving evidence of a decline.

The view of these relics of cloister art convinces us that they of the dark ages did not contribute the truly beautiful.... Yet shadows pass "with time and the hour."... Night is passing, ... comes the gray, ... comes the dawn, ... comes the morning light. Creatures that at evening ceased their song, tune now their pipes and sing again; they chant anon the requiem of the Night of Art; and yet anon, they sing the coming of the light. They celebrate at last, with hope, the renewing of all things beautiful in art. The orb of day gilds the horizon; man beholds the aurora of approaching day.

RENAISSANCE.

In the fifteenth and sixteenth centuries, under the encouragement of the Medici family, skilled artisans again emigrated to Italy as coadjutors in the great revival of all that was beautiful in gem-engraving.

They created, for the glyptic phase of art, a position almost as important as it had enjoyed in the first century A. D.

It is not surprising that comparatively so few engraved gems have been handed down to us when we consider the tides of the last twenty centuries as a great sea which has borne to the shores of civilized Europe, and later to America, specimens of ancient art creations—that sea, at times placid, yet ever and anon turbulent with devastating storms, whose iconoclastic waves broke upon the ancient sites of antiquity, destroying treasures that thus have been irreparably lost to archæological science and to our museums.

As a child becomes restless with the consciousness of coming day before it fully wakes from sleep, man, weary of this night of ignorance and the atmosphere of barbarism— fretful on his couch under the yoke of tyranny, striving to shake it off while yet enveloped by the shades of error, rose up to seek an element he knew not, a light he dreamed would come!

SOMMERVILLE COLLECTION.

624

601

634

632

1358

621

631

616

RENAISSANCE-MEDICI PERIOD.

He burst the cords that bound his strength; he pierced the clouds which dulled his vision, and, leaving his prison-house, reached forth his fearless arm, and pushing aside the sombre folds of the long intervening veil, peered into the outer world of progress, and in the gray gloom he descried a distant terrace. With rapid strides, through furrows of popular prejudice and cinders of past magnificence, over crumbled arch and fallen pillar, frieze, and pediment, he sped his way; nor flagged nor halted, till the summit reached, he stood and gazed with earnest look out into the coming time; he beheld in the vista before him many streams flowing into the sea of the future. In the horizon gleamed again the omen of coming day; it was the harbinger of a new birth.

The light of truth flashed upon his mind, discovering to him his freed intellect. Unlike the denizens of the earlier age of luxury and repletion, he stood a thinking man, refreshed, invigorated, and ready for work; and quickly he applied himself; called forth his kinsman; his voice was heard throughout the land; men awoke everywhere and wrought in the ateliers of the new life.

Through the air came strains as of music, from creaking of timber, cracking of stone, the carol of the painter, hammer and anvil, plashing oar, wheel and shaft, mallet and chisel, and with the new demand upon the gem-engravers came— the Oratorio of the Renaissance.

With this awakening came another influx of skilled artisans into Italy, not to compete, as before, in the great established art market of the world. Now they came in response to appeals for master-workmen, came to instruct, to encourage the new birth; to lead the drowsy ones out into the full light of day, the day of a rising constellation in which once more shone brilliantly a meritorious school of gem-engravers.

Though Germany, France, and other nations shared in the work, Italy guarded the cradle of the Renaissance, and as a faithful, loving parent, watched the developing features of the youth, which grew apace, reading there the promise of a growing power that was destined to lead future generations to excellence and prosperity in art.

Italy accomplished the first great work of this period by furnishing models for both industrial and fine arts, infusing vitality into other nations. The influential families of the Medici and Farnese, Popes Leo X. and Paul III., many cardinals and nobles, were instrumental in the revival of gem-engraving; especially Lorenzo de Medici contributed to its redevelopment and growth by inducing artists to devote themselves to its practice and bestowing on them his liberal patronage.

The vigorous manner of artists of this period is so marked that even in the reproduction of antique designs a connoisseur can recognize their peculiar style. Their original works are highly meritorious, attaining a great degree of excellence. Many rose to eminence; some, not content with rising in the firmanent of the dawning effulgence, aspired to positions in the bright constellation of fame, producing engraved gems for the ornamentation of costumes, armor, inlaying and embossing of vases, tankards, etc.

SUCCEEDING DECLINES AND REVIVALS.

Constant encouragement was given to this branch of art-industry throughout the fifteenth and part of the sixteenth century; but after the death of the Emperor Charles V., in 1558, recurred another period of decline. Private and royal accumulations of art works were again the victims of depredation; cabinets and museums were pillaged and scattered by military marauders, as one after another the great cities of the Continent of Europe were besieged and conquered.

The glyptic, of all the arts, was the most easily affected by the changing fortunes of nations.

These circumstances compelled artists to give their attention more particularly to church architecture, to the production of large devotional basso-rilievos for the altar, and sculptured figures, which, though representing sacred subjects, were often too voluptuous in form, and lacking the essential qualities of true art.

In the last twenty years of the eighteenth century gem-engraving received fresh impetus; new practitioners were enrolled from Germany, England, and France.

Some of these resided many years in England, pursuing their profession assiduously and profitably. In this period quantities of intaglios and cameos were reproduced from the most salable antique subjects. To supply the wants of enthusiastic amateurs frauds were freely committed, by close imitation, and the insertion of signatures of celebrated Greek and Roman engravers, though the age produced artists of the highest ability and honor.

The works of Natter, Sirletti, Pickler, Marchand, Pistrucci, Santarelli, and others come to us so directly from their hands that we feel they almost belong to our day, and we think of them as of acquaintances.

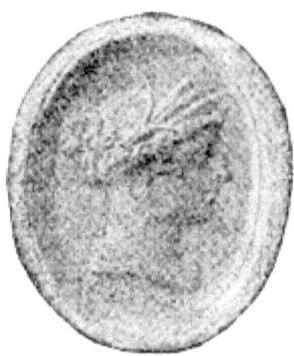

Many of the gems of Giovanni Pickler compare favorably with the finest incisions of the Greek, and even with the work of the renowned Dioscorides.

During the latter part of the eighteenth century and the commencement of the nineteenth, monarchs and noblemen indulged in making collections of gems to such an extent that the list of patrons increased competition, and fabulous prices were obtained from such buyers as the Empress Catherine II. of Russia, the Prince Frederick of Prussia, the Duke of Orleans, George III., the Empress Josephine of France, and many of the English nobility, among others the Dukes of Devonshire and Marlborough.

Almost until now no plea has been offered for glyptology as a factor contributing historical data. The mass of scientists have been contented with musty old volumes, and these little message-bearing stones have been regarded as nothing more than curious ancient articles of luxury, yet you will remark we do not look on them in that light; we recognize, as we justly should, each and every piece as part of a great story, recording and illustrating many epochs and eras in this world's history, and patiently we have been seeking to replace each fragment into its proper place in the inscribed diagram, until we are convinced that we read thereon many things that no manuscripts or books have communicated to us.

SOME TYPES OF REMARKABLE GEMS.

My entire collection in the Free Museum of Science and Art of the University of Pennsylvania must be examined to see types of all these epochs. It may be well to notice here three or four very remarkable gems of which monographs have also been published.

Bacchus and Ariadne.

Ariadne is seated on the rocks of Dia, where Bacchus found her; at her feet is her panther. Bacchus bears in his hand a thrysus; his javelin with its point in the form of a pine cone; his head wreathed with ivy and grape leaves; his hand lovingly placed on sad Ariadne's shoulder, who has just been deserted by Theseus. Bacchus, deeply in love (which is indicated by the figure of Cupid), says to her, "I shall care for thee." The panther at the feet of Ariadne is emblematic of the principal and most important incident in her life, her love for Theseus.

Ariadne was the daughter of Minos, King of Crete. She fell in love with Theseus when he went as one of the seven youths whom the Athenians were obliged to send every year with seven maidens to Crete to be devoured by the Minotaur.

Ariadne provided Theseus with a sword with which he slew the Minotaur, and with a thread which enabled him to find his way out of the labyrinth; they then fled to the island of Naxos (Dia), where Theseus, warned by a god in a dream, deserted her. Bacchus arrived opportunely from India, finding Ariadne in a state of grief and consternation, which even added to her charming beauty; he quenched her tears, consoled her, and took her to himself. This exquisite gem is a fine representation of Renaissance work (see plate on p. 81).

JUPITER ÆGIOCHUS.

Among examples of antique glyptic art, by referring to my late work on "Engraved Gems: Their Place in the History of Art," you will find an extended notice of the superb ancient cameo on chrysoprase of Jupiter Ægiochus. It is the eighth of importance in the remarkable antique cameos that have been preserved from the early centuries after Christ. It is of remarkable dimensions, being 167 millimetres in height by 130 millimetres in breadth.

It is of the close of the epoch of Marcus Aurelius or the earlier years of the reign of Commodus. The style is that of the Græco-Roman art. The work is very beautiful for that epoch, and there rests in this head of the master of the gods an accent of grandeur in which one feels the reflection of the original Greek of the better centuries, imitated here by the engraver of the Græco-Roman age.

SOMMERVILLE COLLECTION.

JUPITER ÆGIOCHUS.

It is an interesting circumstance, which merits particular attention, that the cameo Zulian coming from Ephesus and this Jupiter Ægiochus are certainly of the workmanship of Asia Minor.

Early in this century this cameo made part of the celebrated Northwick Collection of England. Afterwards it was acquired by a wealthy connoisseur in France, and later passed into the possession of M. Feuardent, Paris, when, with his permission, an engraving of it appeared, with five quarto pages of text and notes, in the *Gazette Archæologique*, Paris, 1877, edited by Baron J. De Witte, Membre de l'Institut and François Lenormant.

M. Adrien Longperier, the distinguished glyptologist and savant of the Institut de France, some thirty years ago made a study of this gem, and seriously contemplated its acquisition for France; he urged the French Government to authorize its purchase for the collection in the Salle des Pierres gravées in the Bibliothèque Nationale, Paris, or for the Museum of the Louvre. Several other museums also negotiated for its purchase, but the late owner being firm in his demand, the price caused them to delay, and now it belongs to America, being part of my collection.

THE TRIUMPH OF CONSTANTINE.

Among the most important and interesting antique gems in my collection is one engraved when Constantine held the Roman Empire in Byzantia, which came into the possession of the Court of Russia.

The Empress Catherine II., wishing to confer a great favor and special reward on an ambassador to her court from her remarkable collection in the Museum of the Hermitage at St. Petersburg, presented this antique gem to him in 1785. Twenty-five years afterwards, at his death in Greece, it was sold, and was piously guarded during thirty years by a collector in the Hellenic peninsula. After that it became the property of Bieler in Styria.

I came into possession of this remarkable gem after more

than five years' negotiations with its owner, and subsequently with his heirs.

It is a cameo of great importance in itself. Prof. C. W. King, of Trinity College, Cambridge, England, said, "It is by far the most important of all similar works of the Lower Empire hitherto published."

It is of very considerable dimensions (6 × 4 inches), being the eleventh in point of magnitude of those already existing in any cabinet. It is a maculated sard, dark-reddish amber color, with slight white, dark sepia, and burnt sienna spots or maculation.

The subject is a Triumph of Constantine. This portrait of that Byzantine Emperor is considered very faithful. As I have often remarked in connection with the numismatic phase of my subject, we can in this case establish the likeness of Constantine by confronting it with the fine gold coins of his realm and reign.

Among the auxiliary figures on the gem is Constantine's mother Helena, she who found the true cross; also Crispus his son, and his wife Fausta.

The Emperor is being crowned by a Victory, who stands behind him borne in a triumphal car, the four horses walking and led by a soldier in front. Constantine holds the reins in his left hand, but in his right a roll of paper (volumen), instead of the customary eagle-tipped sceptre.

In the front of the group is a standard inscribed "S. P. Q. R.," the bearer of the staff being concealed by the horses of the car; as are also the lictors, whose fasces are seen elevated in the air above the horses' backs, in the upper field of the composition. Behind the car stands Crispus and Fausta, both in front face; Crispus is pointing to the labarum, and evidently relating to Fausta all the circumstances of its introduction into the scene. At the opposite end of the gem stands Helena, who, with the soldier leading the quadriga, forms a balance to the other pair.

Much labor and skill have been expended by the artist upon the face of the triumphing Cæsar, in order to leave no doubt as to his identity, and with such success that the well-known Augustus-like profile of Constantine may be recognized at the first glance.

RELIGION ON STONES.

We have found here unquestionably information not to be obtained from any other source. If ancient engraved stones had never been unearthed or found, we would have been ignorant to-day of much that is interesting and important concerning the historic chain which now connects us with the traditions of men in the incipiency of art thousands of years before the era of manuscripts.

We hold and esteem the Holy Bible not only as our guide and as the book of God's laws, but also as one of the most perfect compends of the history of the world from all known time. The earliest mention of the profession of gem-cutting is in the thirty-first chapter of Exodus, from the first to the fifth verse, inclusive:

"And the Lord spake unto Moses, saying, See, I have called by name Bezaleel the son of Uri, the son of Hur, of the tribe of Judah: and I have filled him with the spirit of God, in wisdom, and in understanding, and in knowledge, and in all manner of workmanship, to devise cunning works, to work in gold, and in silver, and in brass, and in cutting of stones, to set them," etc., "and to work in all manner of workmanship." This commission was for the Jews to adorn the ark of the testimony and to attach to the Esod a part of the vestiture of the grand sacerdotal of the Israelites. Our observation of this branch of art has been strictly in accordance with our intended plan.

We have regarded almost solely all these beautiful stones in the light of art, with a view of considering their comparative art-merits; yet I have always seen in their history another and somewhat important phase, to me an interesting one: that is, their connection with the traditions, legends, and annals of religion. We find on them tenets of paganism, mysticism, mythology, and the Christian religion—symbols, dogmas, and pictured revelations of creeds of many nations and of people almost otherwise unknown—what may indeed be classified as religious stone-literature.

Skilful utilization of the colored strata and maculation of onyxes and agates depict fire and water as objects of adoration; altars rendered sacred by their inscriptions, each with its patron god upon it or hovering near; characters there inscribed telling to whose service they were dedicated —now to a supreme being beloved, though absent; again, to a deity adored, though unseen.

Every tribe seems to have had a Father above, though we do not meet with the vague superscription, "To the unknown God."

On every side objects of veneration: the heavens; innumerable mention of deities dwelling therein; plenteous aspirations and appeals to their clemency, forbearance, and protection.

These talismanic gems, whenever they are religiously inscribed, I treasure as tablets of faith—a faith which, though often erroneously placed, was fervent and abiding as it was indelibly registered.

Rambling in many strange countries, seeing palaces, costumes, men, and manners, this subject, paramount to them all, has often received my attention—a theme the most precious to the scattered races of the human family, their religion. It is worthy of remark that so large a proportion of the intaglios and seals were of a religious character.

The ancient residents near the sea and on all the frontier of Asia Minor had their religious token-gems.

In this day of enlightenment naturally we are astonished that men could have believed in these gods or in such theories and dogmas, and expressing astonishment that they could have trusted in these talismans or hoped for benefits from them. We wonder at the absurd codes of mythological religion; yes, let us call it so; that is what it was for these people; they knew not our God, they had never heard of our divine Master.

Until the revelation of Christ to us, man naturally had to look somewhere for refuge for his soul; he had to cling to some unseen hand, lest he should fall.

Do we often realize what modern Christianity is? These pagans, of whose religions we have so many little stone monuments, were all anterior to and existed during ages before that revelation.

Christians of to-day, reflect: all these heathen, as you no doubt esteem them, were earnest in the performance of their duties, their prayers, their adoration, and their sacrifices — many of them more devout than some of us under the light of the twentieth century.

True, these religions were the inventions of men, the outcome of the longings and yearnings of sympathetic men for a superior guiding and protecting power — Deity, if you will allow it — to which to turn and in which to hope.

They worshipped faithfully, adored sincerely, obeyed implicitly, lived simple lives, in keeping with their primitive faith. Was it not reasonable, this worship of a people who had no divine revelation? Was it not beautiful? Can you not even now see something to admire in devotional exercises held in God's open air, turning in adoration myriads of earnest eyes upon the Sun, "the beauty and the glory of the day," devoutly praising from the heart the majesty and the power of the Supreme Being, the Maker and the Ruler of this benign light? Their principal fête, on which they all assembled joyfully and gratefully to bow before the glorious orb, was on the same day we have accepted as the anniversary of the birth of Christ our Redeemer.

And so it was with those who venerated and carried engraved emblems of those incomprehensible elements, Fire and Water.

As symbolic of the inscrutable power the Parsees keep a flame constantly burning upon an altar in the inner temple; so sacred is it that only the higher priests set apart for that service can enter therein; yet through their mediation thousands participate in the ceremony and enjoy the consolation of its power — a force of terrible destructibility, yet with the genial phase which comforts and contributes to the nourishment of man. This form of worship originated in Persia, and when its disciples emigrated and distributed themselves throughout many countries and islands of India and the shores of the neighboring seas, they carefully carried the sacred fire with them; and it is believed it has never ceased to burn during many centuries. Red and spotted maculation in agates have been utilized by incisori to represent the flame of an altar fire.

Even to this day many of these objects in stone are treasured and valued by men and women in secluded villages in the East; they hold and guard them as religious heirlooms. I have bartered with them successfully, and have bought their bracelets, finger-rings, and nose-rings; yet so highly have these sacred talismans been esteemed that those which I most desired have rarely and only with difficulty been obtained from their superstitious possessors.

In the two or three centuries succeeding the advent of Christ the Abraxas flourished and engraved the mass of religious mystic talismans (already described in their place in this book). Their priests or pastors, in the term accepted by us, prepared these amulets, engraving upon them attributes and symbols of the Most High; they taught their followers to wear them close to their hearts, these reminders of their heavenly Father, these rude glyptic lights that kept them nearer to God. I do not, cannot, find it absurd. When you have considered this subject as now presented, you will perhaps view with new interest these devotional tokens, after many years of travel and research brought together and classified in my cabinet.

HISTORIC CAMEOS.

A large class of ancient seems were historical. In my collection may be found a series of cameos, all works of the most able artists of the epoch of Trajan, which are now esteemed in Rome as works of the highest merit.

They portray the pleasures of the hunting expeditions, the wars, and other incidents in the life of Trajan and Titus Vespasianus.

These cameos were the subjects of the *basso-rilievos* which ornamented a triumphal arch erected in honor of Trajan.

In the reign of the Emperor Constantine the Romans despoiled this monument of all these subjects tributary to Trajan, and adorned with them the arch which they then built for Constantine. It was said in those days no emperor had ever equalled Constantine in building up the Empire, and therefore they did not hesitate to dismantle a monument of his predecessor.

SOMMERVILLE COLLECTION.

1347

1348

HISTORICAL CAMEOS.

An interesting historic cameo is Coriolanus visited by his mother Veturia and his wife Volumnia. His original name was Marcius, but on account of his valor in a contest against the Volscians he was surnamed Coriolanus. In the time of a famine he was impeached for his opinions in regard to the distribution of corn received from Sicily; he was condemned to exile. He now went over to the Volscians, and became general of their army, and successfully attacked the Romans; they, fearing him, made advances to him and offered the restoration of all his property and franchises; he resisted all their propositions. It was not until his mother and wife came to him that he could be induced to relent; their prayers and tears, however, moved him; he then retired with his army, but passed the remainder of his life with the Volscians, who had honored him for his valor and not from fear. The guard with a shield at the right is a Volscian, and he at the left is a Roman.

Observe in my collection an allocution of Marcus Aurelius before the Prætorian Guard: the guard are not only known by their costume, but by the banner which is marked S. C. (*Senatus Consultum*).

No incidents in ancient history are more interesting or more dramatic than the episodes in the life and career of fair Cleopatra; one of the most vivid to my fancy's recollection is the scene of her fatal giving up of that romantic life as depicted on a beautiful turquoise cameo—No. 346.

It is well understood that many of the cameos concerning Christ are truly historical. There is also Horatius defending the bridge. The bridge was on the Tiber at Rome; Horatius was fighting the Etruscans; the Romans were obliged to destroy their end of the bridge, when Horatius with his horse swam back.

True, we have history through classic Latin sources of the most important events of the first and second centuries. Yet these portraitures on stone, executed in the very epochs, add certainly great interest to the records of these times. The subjects on stone alluded to, mirror to us more faithfully, more vividly, scenes in the lives of several Roman emperors than any manuscript possibly could have done.

We have Trajan as emperor, judge, and warrior. We see him engaged in conflict, we admire him victorious, we rejoice in his happy return to Rome on several occasions; in his triumphant reception both by the people and the army, and in the arches erected as souvenirs of his prowess; in his dignified reception of the son of the King of the Armenians, and in his condescension in restoring their kingdom; in several of his expeditions against the Dacians, and in his happy escape from the plot of Decebalus. We have instances of his public charities delicately depicted in cameo; his religious sacrifices; his exploits as a hunter of many wild animals, the boar and the lion included, are exemplified. We have several beautiful groups with emperors delivering allocutions before the cohorts of their armies, senators, and other dignitaries; the triumphant entry of Titus Vespasianus into Jerusalem, whereon twenty-two figures are visible, and the exit from Jerusalem of his victorious army, on which nineteen figures are seen; also the groups of Jewish prisoners.

All these pages in my stone book are certainly interesting additions to ancient history.

SOMMERVILLE COLLECTION.

1339

1350   1351

1349

HISTORICAL CAMEOS.

ANIMALS AND BIRDS.

We have seen how large a proportion of the subjects on ancient gems were mythological, how extended was the class of religious and of Christian subjects; we have noted the loved portraits of sovereigns, statesmen, philosophers, physicians, and poets.

There remains a series worthy of notice—those intaglios and cameos worn as amulets on which were engraved innumerable animals, birds, fishes, and even insects.

As the families of the nobility chose the insignia which entered into the quarterings of their escutcheons, so the ancients according to their superstitions or their tastes chose some patron animal or bird for an emblem and caused it to be engraved on their talismans; and these symbols were cherished with what might almost be termed religious fervency.

They were used as amulets, supposed to protect the wearers against accident and to repel danger. There was almost a pharmacopœia of gems, with solace for every trouble of mind and a remedy for every disease.

A dolphin, the mariner's friend, on sard or carnelian, was an emblem worn by fishermen, and was believed to protect them from the attacks of sharks or other voracious fishes. They also carried with equal reliance the same design in antique paste.

The eagle of Jupiter is symbolic of his power, although it was subservient to him. This no doubt accounts for its appropriation in heraldry by sovereigns.

The raven, the friend of Apollo; the parrot, a loquacious inebriate, is often an attendant on Bacchus.

The aringa, a fish of the Adriatic Sea, represented on a talisman in my collection, was worn by women on account of its being the symbol of fruitfulness; it deposits many thousand eggs each year.

Certain insects, arachnids, and reptiles were employed as symbols, because they were supposed to protect man in each case from the enemy thereon delineated.

A scorpion on a transparent stone was an amulet against the sting of the arachnid.

As the scorpion inflicts a painful sting, the spider a venomous bite, and a variety of flies make dangerous aggression on the human form, their images engraved on stones were believed to shield the wearer from the ills due to attacks from corresponding insects.

One of the most minute insects employed as a talisman is the ant, symbolic of industry.

The peacock frequently appears on gems; naturally, no one would have had it as an emblem of vanity, in which sense it is generally accepted in modern times, but it was revered as the favorite of Juno.

The owl: Minerva's head is at times draped with an owl; its connection with Minerva is that it is symbolic of profound meditation.

Beautiful storks occur frequently on engraved gems: they were so abundant in Asia Minor and in the Byzantine

Empire that husbandmen sought to frighten them away; yet in other lands they were almost adored. In modern Fünen, and generally in Scandinavia, storks building their nests on the roofs of houses in the country are welcomed as bringing children for the household, and are cared for with a credulity equalling pagan superstition.

The frog has sometimes found a place in Christian symbolism as the most expressive image of the resurrection of the body, because frogs, like the serpents after their winter interment, emerge from their hiding-places and renew their youth by casting their slough.

Many farm and house companions figure in the series: a dog, fidelity; a cock, vigilance; a turtle, always at home; a snail, there is no hurry; a sheep, humility; a lamb, innocence; a horse, patience and endurance; a dove, harmless, the Holy Spirit; a lion, majesty and force; a serpent, wisdom, and, with its tail in mouth, eternity; a serpent was often represented on the stone above the fireplace in Roman kitchens; a ram was significant of the Nundine sacrifices made weekly to Jupiter; a lion and a goat driven by Cupid, the power of love: he guides not only the lascivious, but the strong.

ANTIQUE PASTES.

The Antique Pastes are interesting from the fact that they present us with many curious mythological subjects not always to be found on semi-precious stones. They are specimens of a branch of early Roman industry.

They were made in imitation of Oriental stones, of which the supply was inadequate for the great demand of the first and second centuries A. D., and also as a matter of economy. Often in ancient times a quantity of fragments of hard semi-precious pebbles too small to be engraved were pulverized, and the sand or granulated mass was fused in crucibles just as glass is made. This process enabled many lovers of the art to possess examples in this cheaper artificial substance when the same subjects on real India stones were commanding exorbitant prices. Some of these gems are beautifully opalescent and iridescent.

This iridescence, though so beautiful on the specimens of that kind, is only owing to chemical action on the paste gems during the centuries they have been buried in the earth. Interesting intaglios and cameos in enamel have withstood the wear of ages, and are in better condition; the imitations of red jasper are wonderful.

SOMMERVILLE COLLECTION.

1183

1244

105

ANTIQUE PASTES.

Many intaglios in antique paste are representations in designs of ancient bronzes, of which we have no other trace except their mention by early historians.

The most precious antique example in paste is the Portland Vase. It was discovered in the sixteenth century in a sarcophagus within the monument of the Emperor Alexander Severus and his mother, Julia Mamæa, on the Frascati road, about two miles and a half from Rome. It was long known as the Barberini Vase, having belonged to that family in Rome for two hundred years; thence it came to England in the last century, and after twice changing ownership, at the death of the Duchess of Portland, from whom it takes its name, it was sold to the Duke of Marlborough, and is now in the British Museum. It has been broken and mended. It is about ten inches high, and at the broadest part six inches in diameter. It was formed of paste, and afterward engraved.

The paste is in imitation of onyx, in two strata, white upon blue, of an amethyst tinge; the figures are cut in relief on the lighter color, the blue forming the second plane or background.

Though the antique paste cameos and intaglios are largely reproductions of subjects also found engraved on pietradura, we are indebted to this class of gems for many examples of ancient cameos and intaglios which we would otherwise never have seen; in fact, from the rare beauty of some specimens in paste, they never could have existed in any other material.

Not only do both intaglios and cameos in antique paste present us with the choicest examples of miniature art, but the iridescence created on them by time frequently renders them the most beautiful specimens in a collection.

MYTHOLOGICAL.

Through the possession of these Pagan cameos and intaglios we have become heirs to the most thorough knowledge of Mythology.

Hundreds of distinct specimens may be gathered from glyptic work centuries before Christ, and so arranged as to form several genealogical trees.

In Mythology there is not one single ancestor of all, as in the biblical history, where Adam is honored with being our original and only progenitor and equally censured with being the testator of our legacy of all human ills. The myriad bigamist ancestors of the countless mythological beings pictured on ancient gems have created and bequeathed to us numerous families of celestial and terrestrial divinities, denizens of earth, air, and water, and hundreds of grotesque chimeras.

Like the royal families of our sphere, there was much intermarriage of close relatives, many of their offspring bearing at times the forms of animals, birds, and anon reptiles. Some of their descendants were even metamorphosed in those tropical climes into trees, under the cooling umbrage of which other scions were born and commenced their adventurous career.

These poetical conceptions were the mythological forerunners of the simpler, purer, diviner religion which was eventually given to man. A close observer may find in these legendary myths antetypes of the omnipotent Godhead now revealed to us and in which is our sure hope and trust.

CHINESE, BURMESE, AND SIAMESE.

The Chinese are the only race producing glyptic work in relief on hard Jade, and also on stones resembling it—in which one is easily deceived.

They are said to be good copyists: all designs given to them for reproduction are copied very closely, but in what we find on engraved stones there is the type of their nationality; it resembles nothing else. Their work is mostly in very low relief, on Nacre, Jade, Amethyst, and Agalmatolite.

Their pictured stones generally represent hideous animals, birds, fruits, and views of paradise with figures of grotesque divinities. Their inscriptions are not deeply incised, but are usually letters or characters in their language in relief.

The exquisitely beautiful details often exhibited by the Chinese are surprising, especially when we consider the hardness of the Jade, the material principally employed by them.

What patience it must have required to cut those ornaments in Jade which we find on their scepters and on the handles of their official swords! Many pieces which are shown in museums have cost years of laborious engraving. Jade has therefore been esteemed by the Chinese as emblematic of all virtue.

In this connection it may be remarked that the Burmese and the Siamese have seldom engraved on any stones harder than Alabaster or Agalmatolite (Chinese figure stone). Their subjects principally represent Buddha; occasionally his two feet; their emblematic flowers, and their deeply-revered sacred Bôdhi-tree at Gaya.

SOMMERVILLE COLLECTION.

659

AZTEC.

AZTEC OR MEXICAN.

The American Continent has contributed some unique work executed by the Aztecs anterior to the Spanish conquest of Mexico.

Among the existing glyptic relics of nations we find no examples of execution in stone-engraving more peculiar than what has been preserved of the work of the Aztecs or Mexicans, especially that done before the occupation by Pizarro.

The character of their work is so crude and distinct that no close observer can for a moment be mistaken in detecting its origin.

I have met with Aztec engraved stones among a miscellaneous collection offered to me for selection; there was that quality which enables a connoisseur to recognize the class of ornamentation doubtless worn by that people whom Prescott represented as decorated principally by gold, silver, and feathers.

Large pieces, cameos of two and a half to three inches, have been found which were worn by the Incas as breast ornaments, and are always pierced, which shows that they were suspended from the neck.

In fact, some of the most faithful representations of costume, head-dress, and weapons are in *basso-rilievo* engraved stones in opaque white Alabaster and pale-green hard Nephrite.

RETROSPECTIVE.

We have much to enjoy as we survey the gems of the various epochs. The multifarious types that have been gathered in forty centuries meet our view, grouped in the tableau of engraved gems.

Our attention is drawn with interest to each sentiment expressed, feature defined, or emotion portrayed. We study the diversified qualities—the fineness or freedom of touch, ingenious effects, delicate lines, choice attitudes, graceful forms, force, spirit, and tenderness—which characterize these monuments of patience.

The engraved gems rescued from the torrent, ebbing and flowing with the fluctuating fortunes of ages, garnered by successive generations, enrich the traditional viaduct traversing the morass of many centuries. Some blocks are less beautiful than others in the structure, but from them we have founded our first footholds, and from them we mount to the work that embellishes the great Etruscan arches even when we revel on the finely pencilled coping-stones of the Greek and Roman epochs, or admire the ornate abutments of the Renaissance, we should revert with pleasure to the earlier, ruder contributions in the foundations, and we can find pleasure in viewing and studying every part.

The builder's stones are graven—the footway is of pictured pebbles, miniatures, amulets, and seals, reflecting lineaments and traces of the history of entombed generations. Their inscriptions reveal to us the impress of ancient, mediæval, and modern art.

INDEX.